*For Alannah and Luisa
with love from Dad*

*For Ellanuuna the ballerina
from Chantal*

The Dance Teacher

Words *by* Simon Milne

Pictures *by* Chantal Stewart

ALLEN & UNWIN
SYDNEY · MELBOURNE · AUCKLAND · LONDON

Miss Sylvie had a dance studio just over the bridge.

Every Saturday she listened for the sound
of feet on the path. A few minutes later,
the studio door would open and
her students would rush in.

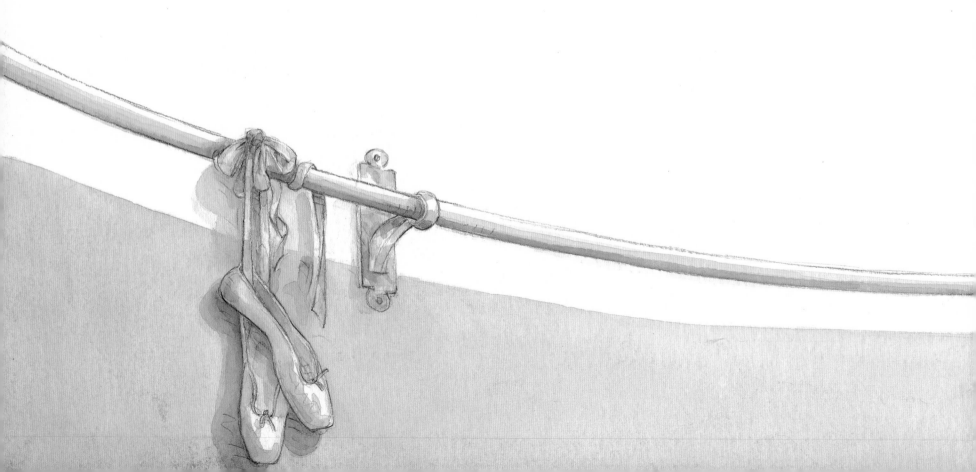

In the morning she taught
a junior ballet class.

At lunchtime she taught an
intermediate hip-hop class.

And in the afternoon she taught
a senior jazz and tap class.

'Teaching is the best job in the world,'
Miss Sylvie always said.

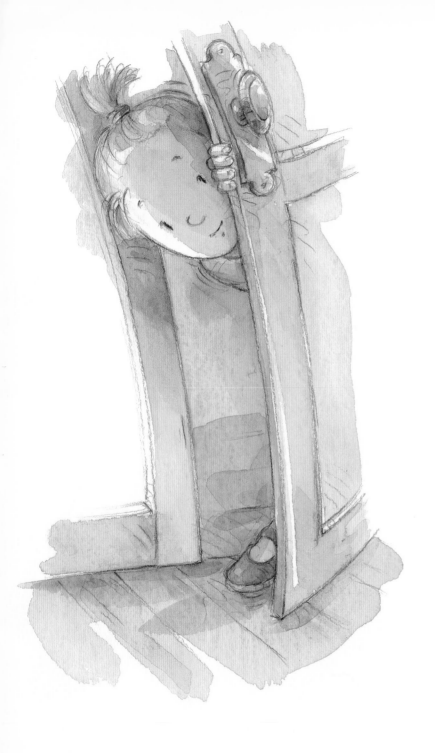

One weekend Miss Sylvie was practising
at the barre when a little girl peered
around the studio door.

'Hello,' said Miss Sylvie.
'Hello,' said the little girl.
'I am Isabelle.
I want to be a ballerina.'

'Dancing is hard work. You have to practise every week.
Are you ready to work hard?' asked Miss Sylvie.
Isabelle nodded.

So Isabelle joined Miss Sylvie's junior ballet class.
She practised the five positions:

first

second

third

fourth

and fifth.

The next year all the ballet students joined the hip-hop class –
except Isabelle and her two friends, Holly and Sarah.
'We want to keep doing ballet,' Isabelle said.
'Don't you want to join the hip-hop class with all your other friends?' asked Miss Sylvie.
Isabelle nodded. 'But we want to be ballerinas more than anything.'

So Miss Sylvie let them join her weeknight classes.

The three girls practised over and over again.
They learned *plié, arabesque, glissé* and *pas de chat*.
This was Isabelle's favourite – the step of the cat.

Sometimes the girls had to rest because of their injuries.
Sometimes they had to miss birthday parties.
But they never missed Miss Sylvie's ballet class.

Then life got in the way for the three girls.

Holly no longer had
time for ballet.

Sarah joined the
hockey team.

Only Isabelle kept going.
Day after day, week after week…and year after year.

The time came when Isabelle was ready for *pointe* work.
She took Miss Sylvie's hand…

…and went up on *pointe* for the first time!

Then she danced across the studio floor on her own.
She felt beautiful and strong and free.
Miss Sylvie was so proud.
Isabelle was a ballerina at last!

One day Isabelle was accepted into the Dance Academy in the city.
She and Miss Sylvie wrote to each other every week.

As her dancing improved,
Isabelle joined the *Corps de Ballet*.
Over time she became a soloist,
then a principal,
then…

...a prima ballerina.

Miss Sylvie was the
proudest teacher ever.

Isabelle danced all around the world for many years.
She loved being a ballerina.

One day, many years later, Isabelle
knew that she was ready to stop.
'I am tired,' she said to herself.
'I want to go home.'

The first thing Isabelle did when she
got home was cross the bridge
to Miss Sylvie's dance studio.

Miss Sylvie was sitting in her chair
when a familiar face peered around
the studio door.
'Isabelle!'

Isabelle and Miss Sylvie gave each other the biggest hug ever.
'I am ready to become a teacher,' said Isabelle.
'Are you sure?' Miss Sylvie said.
Isabelle nodded.

So Isabelle bought the dance studio from Miss Sylvie.

Now she teaches the morning junior ballet class,
the lunchtime intermediate hip-hop class and
the afternoon senior jazz and tap class.
At the end of each day, she sits down in her chair to rest.
'Teaching is the best job in the world,'
she says to herself.

And one day a little girl peers
through the studio door…

First published in 2013

Allen & Unwin
83 Alexander Street
Crows Nest NSW 2065
Australia
Phone: (61 2) 8425 0100
Email: info@allenandunwin.com
Web: www.allenandunwin.com

A Cataloguing-in-Publication entry is available
from the National Library of Australia
www.trove.nla.gov.au

ISBN 978 1 74331 331 2

Cover and text design by Sandra Nobes and Chantal Stewart
Set in 18 pt Berkeley Oldstyle by Sandra Nobes
Colour reproduction by Splitting Image, Clayton, Victoria
This book was printed in April 2013 at Hang Tai Printing (Guang Dong) Ltd.,
Xin Cheng Ind Est, Xie Gang Town, Dong Guan, Guang Dong Province, China

1 3 5 7 9 10 8 6 4 2